Sweet Dominique

Sweet Dominique

WILL HOLMES

iUniverse®

SWEET DOMINIQUE

iUniverse books may be ordered through booksellers or by contacting:

iUniverse
1663 Liberty Drive
Bloomington, IN 47403
www.iuniverse.com
1-800-Authors (1-800-288-4677)

ISBN: 978-1-5320-9023-3 (sc)
ISBN: 978-1-5320-9022-6 (e)

Print information available on the last page.

iUniverse rev. date: 05/23/2020

INTRODUCTION

Will Holmes I was born in New Orleans Louisiana, although I was raised in Thibodaux Louisiana. My mother and father was raised on a plantation farm in Napoleonville, Louisiana. My parents would get married and bring forth seven kids. Me, being the oldest. My Southern Louisiana roots are deep. I developed my story telling talents from listening to older people tell stories about the older days as a little boy. I developed and sharpened my writing skills from writing music for over twenty years as a musical artist. Sweet Dominique was derived from a song I wrote twenty years ago. I later expanded it to a screenplay. Several years later I received a vision to release Sweet Dominique as a book. I left Sweet Dominique in quasi, screenplay writing form so my readers could authentically see my vision better.. My goal in this book was to give knowledge, wisdom and educate others. While using story, telling. With realistic energy. I love people and I want to do my part to inspire and help others get through adversity all over the world. After reading this book I advise that you shoot for the stars and on your journey help someone else along the way.

Thomas is rushing his wife to the hospital emergency doors; as his wife has labor pains
Thomas: I need a doctor. I think her water bag just bust!

Nurse: Sir, What's her name?

Thomas: Evette Lovely

Nurse: Her address and date of birth; is this her first child?

Thomas: Yes, ma'am

Nurse: Please ma'am sit in the wheel chair. Are you in pain?

Evette: YES!

Nurse: Room 414… Put on this robe Mrs. Evette, I'll be back in a moment. Just relax okay.

Evette: Thanks

Hours pass as Thomas walks back and forth. Finally, Evette's two friends come.

Ebony: Thomas how is Evette?

Thomas: She doing well.

Sheila: Can we see her? Thomas: Not at the moment Sheila: Why not?

Thomas: They're running some test on her Ebony: Test!??

The doctor walks in

Doctor: I need to talk to Mr. Thomas, okay.

Ebony and Sheila give Thomas and the doctor some space to talk

Doctor: I have some good news and some bad news. The good news is the baby is healthy. The bad news is your wife can't have this baby. We will have to take the baby. You will have a difficult decision to make as a husband and a father. One of them will not make it the baby or the wife. You have to decide which one of the two will live.

Thomas: No, says Thomas as he begins to sob and cry. Lord this can't be true.

Thomas goes to talk to Evette. He finds her singing a Gospel song

Evette: Thomas I want her to live. She deserves a chance at life.

Thomas: Baby no I want both of you to live. I want us to be a family.

Evette: Raise our child Thomas she will be special. I will name her Sweet Dominique.

SCENE CHANGE

Dominique walking home from school, talking to her friend Stacey

Dominique: My real mom died having me. My dad got married and had my lil' brother, Thomas Jr we called him Tete. He was a straight A student. He cried once because he had a B on his report card once.

Stacey: Wow!

Dominique: Okay I'll see you in the morning.

Stacey: Bye Dominique

SCENE CHANGE

Thomas and Tasha on the phone

Thomas: Hello Tasha how it's going in there this time?

Tasha: Same ole same ole. I've done these 12 step many times. I miss you and Sweet Dominique.

Thomas: I know you do honey but you have to get it right this time, I love you and miss you too.

SCENE CHANGE

Two guys in a car talking

Guy #1: There go that fool right there, let's get him. We ole him

They approach from behind shooting an AK, shooting their target and killing Tete as he was walking home by accident.

SCENE CHANGE

Dominique is dreaming. Pastor preaching, Thomas and Dominique crying in church.

Tasha didn't even show for her son funeral.

Narrator: Tasha would only come home for a day or so and even my dad started acting strange after my lil brother got killed.

SCENE CHANGE

Teacher: Student of the month is Dominique Lovely.

Class claps

After class, teacher and Dominique talk

Teacher: Your grades are going up I am so proud of you Dominique.

Dominique: Yes, my brother have been motivation. I gotta do it for Tete.

Teacher: Keep up the good work Dominique.

SCENE CHANGE

Thomas takes lunch break. Drinking alcohol on his lunch break. Supervisor: Thomas what are you doing? You been in that stall for an hour, lunch been over 30 minutes ago.

Thomas: I will be there in a minute. I have an upset stomach while nervously disposing of the bottle and alcohol.

SCENE CHANGE

Dominique is in the library thinking about when she and Tete was kids.

Tete: Dominique, why my mom always gone?

Dominique: I don't know. What kind of cereal do you want?

Tete: Frosty Flake

Steven: Hey are you all right?

Dominique: Yes.

Steven: You look like you were in a daze. Can I carry your books Dominique: No, I have two hands.

Steven: Are you really that mean?

Dominique: I don't trust people

Steven: Everyone's not here to harm you; I means I will carry your books, buy you lunch, whatever you need me to do. I simply adore you.

Dominque: *Blushes in amazement.*

SCENE CHANGE

Steven: **Daps friend Trevon.** Whats up are you ready for basketball season?

Steven: Hell yeah! Son we gonna have college scouts and coaches at our games, I know to see nigga.

Trevon: Son, they coming to see you too.

Steven: They are coming to see you to fool your the number two small forward in the whole country. Our starting five is going to play college ball.

Trevon: Yea, we gonna be good.

Steven: Hey you remember that mean girl everyone call sweet Dominique? .... I got her to talk to me.

Trevon: Get out of here. She's beautiful and mean. I wish you luck with that one, alright yo.

SCENE CHANGE

Trevon talking to the big dealer in hood.

Knocking on the door

Girl: *opens door*

Two sexy females search Trevon

Trevon: I like this shit, that's why I like doing business here.

Girl: He in the back.

Trevon: Ok

Trevon daps Big Homie

Big Homie: What's good fool, how's school?

Trevon: It's good getting ready for the season.

Big Homie: Yea, I have a $50,000 bet with one of the homies that y'all win state. Don't let me down.

Trevon: We won't. I need some work.

Big Homie: What you need?

Trevon: ***pulls out money*** I need four ounces of that boy, nine ounces of that girls

Big Homie: Hey Domino

Domino: yea

Big Homie: get me four… Hurrican

Hurrican: Yea Daddy

Big Homie: get me nine of that white girl

Hurrican: I got you

Big Homie: ***hands Trevon the product*** Be careful, I got money on yall.

Trevon: Alright bro, I will. My career on the line.

SCENE CHANGE

Dominique washing dishes at home. Her dad, Thomas, is laid back in a chair watching TV. Dominique walks over to her dad and kisses her dad.

Dominique: Dad I need a dress for Prom

Thomas: Okay you just keep your grades up

Dominique: I will, all A's and one B.

Thomas: Alright. Get ready for school tomorrow

Thomas takes a swig of a bottle he had hidden in between his leg and the chair. He then looks up at his son's picture in bitterness and anger.

SCENE CHANGE

Dominique walking to school alone as Steven walks up behind her snatching her bag.

Steven: I told you I would carry your books every day.

Dominique: Oh my you scared me.

Steven: I'm sorry boo. How are you doing this morning?

Dominique: I am doing good. It's kind of chilly out here. I miss judged the temperature.

Steven: Here you can wear my jacket.

Dominique: No then what you gonna wear?

Steven: I have an extra jacket in my locker.

Dominique: Well ok

Steven: Do you have a date for Prom?

Dominique: no I don't

Steven: Well will you be my date?

Dominique: Well, you're like the fourth person to ask me. Let me think about it.

Steven: Okay, just let me know. Here go your books go. That jacket looks so good on you.
    Dominique: *Smiles*

Girl #1: Oh I see you Dominique, that's you?

Dominique: Steven and I are just friends

Girl #2: uuummmmmhhhh

SCENE CHANGE

Steven is walking up to Trevon at his locker

Steven: What's up fool? Damn you always got money and a nice car at school.

Trevon: My parents both have good jobs. They buy me everything as long as I am good in school.

Steven: Oh, first practice tomorrow… be on time. You know Coach Glen will run us to death
    if we're late.

Trevon: I will be on time

Steven: I will talk to you later in Mr. Pete class.

SCENE CHANGE

Phone rings

Coach Glen: Hello

Ben Norway (recruiter) Hi this is Ben Norway from Kentucky Bishop University. I am in the area on a recruiting trip and I would like to know could I come to one of your practices to check out a couple of your kids.

Coach Glen: Well I don't normally do that.

Ben Norway (recruiting): Well would $5,000 change your policy?

Coach Glen: Yes. Our practice start tomorrow at 5:00 pm Ben Norway (recruiting): Okay I will be there with cash. Coach Glen: I will see you there.

SCENE CHANGE

Thomas in the dope trap looking for his wife Tasha Thomas: Hey whats up have you seen Tasha?

Dope Trap Person #1: Yeah I seen her two days ago with this white girl in a Grey Charger.

SCENE CHANGE

Thomas walking the streets looking for Tasha

SCENE CHANGE

Coach Glen is preparing to start practice his high school basketball team.

Ben Norway walks up to Coach Glen

Ben Norway (recruiting): Trevon and Steven is on our radar.

Coach Glen: Yes, they are both talented kids. Many schools have contacted me about them.

Ben Norway gives Coach Glen an envelope

Ben Norway: Thanks I'll be around at games.

Coach Glen: Okay. Just don't approach my kids unless you set up a recruiting visit with their parent.

Ben Norway: Yes, that's the plan

SCENE CHANGE

Back to Thomas. He is sitting in his truck across the street looking for Tasha.

Thomas sees a lady that looks like Tasha. He gets out and approaches her Thomas: Tasha ….is that you?

Tasha: THOMAS **she screams in fear**

Thomas hugs her and knocks the drugs out of her hand.

Thomas: You're coming home!!

Thomas grabs Tasha's arm and pulls her to his truck.

SCENE CHANGE

Narrator: *(Dominique's voice)* The most amazing thing I ever seen daddy convince Tasha to change her life; They went to counseling and church and they both got clean and it was looking normal. I was still missing Tete though.

SCENE CHANGE

Dominique and Steven are walking to the park and talking.

Steven: So Dominique…..... do you have any siblings?

Dominique: The only one I had, he got killed walking home from school; my lil brother Tete.

Steven: Sorry to hear that

Dominique: So what about you?

Steven: I am an only child; been traveling my whole life.

Dominique: Why?

Steven: My dad in the military before I was born.

Dominique: So what about now, are yall settle here?

Steven: Yes my mom and dad divorced a year ago. My mom loves New Orleans i do too. The food is delicious. The crawfish gumbo i love the beignets.

Dominique starts to drift off, thinking about her birth.

Steven: What's wrong? Are you alright?

Dominique: To have a mom, I never met my mom.

Steven: Whhhaaaaaaat? Was you a foster child?

Dominique: NO. my mom died at birth having me.

Steven: Oh my. Wow

Steven hugs Dominique

Dominique starts to cry

Dominique: that's why I been so distant and bitter and angry. I would do anything to have a mom.

Steven: Well, I would share my mom with you. She is adorable.

Dominique: Thanks Steven.

Steven and Dominique kiss and cares each other.

SCENE CHANGE

School Auditorium.

There are football and basketball players athletes.

The famous players come to the school to talk to the athletes

Famous Player: How many of you wanna play professional ball? Raise your hand?

Almost everyone raises their hand

Famous Player: OK that's pretty much everybody. I went to this school seven (7) years ago. I wanna tell you to continue to dream. You can do anything. Although the reality is only a small percentage make it. Think, what is my back up plan. Education is important, work hard in class just like you work hard in sports. They go hand in hand, you can't do one without the other. Continue your dream fellas, it's a lot of distractions for you guys. Although, you have to stay focus,on your goals. Followers let other people think for them. Leaders think for their selves I am donating one hundred and fifty thousand dollars to my school for better equipment and facilities. All in attendance clapped and cheered.

Steven: Hey can I get your autograph?

Famous Player: Of course, I am coming to watch yall play tonight. Do ya thing Steven.

Steven: Wow! He know, my name. We are gonna do our best to win tonight.

SCENE CHANGE

The basketball team won BIG

Score board reads 89-61

Their record is 17-0

Cheerleader highlights; Basketball highlights

SCENE CHANGE

Trevon meets Big Homie in the hood.

Big Homie: Yall doing good bro. 17-0, yall balling nigga.

Trevon: Thanks Big Homie

Big Homie: Keep people out your business. Don't keep a lot of money on you at school. You already riding fly. That's a lot of attention for a high school

Trevon: For sho Big Homie. I got $50,000 grand. I will invest everything I got.

Big Homie: Na homie, never do that. You got to keep bond money stashed.

Give me $40,000 thousand I got you though.

Trevon: Nice looking out

Big Homie: Come through later, I got you and pick up your package.

Trevon: Ok

SCENE CHANGE

Tasha: Hello Honey, how was work?

Thomas: It was great, we got off a hour early so I beat the traffic.

Tasha: I have some good news, I got accepted in the Nursing School.

Thomas: That's Wonderful!

Tasha: That mean I am gonna need my own car because I have to go the work then school.

Thomas: I will start looking for something small, a gas saver.

Did Dominque make it in yet?

Tasha: She in her room.

Thomas walks to Dominique's room. He finds Dominique sitting on the bed on the computer.

Thomas: Hi baby girl.

Dominique: Hey daddy, I didn't know you was here. You're home early.

Thomas: I got off a hour early.

Dominique: I need to talk to you about something.

Thomas: Yes, what's up?

Dominique: I have someone I want you to meet.

Thomas: Who? Steven, the basketball star at your school, what about him?

Dominique: Wow! Daddy I want you to meet him. How you knew that?

Thomas: Okay bring him over. I know everything, I am a parent.

Dominique: Daddy be nice.

Thomas: I will do my best.

SCENE CHANGE

Trevon: *knocks on door before Big Homie trap house*

Security Girl: Who is it?

Trevon: Me

Security Girl opens the door

Two girls pat Trevon down. He has a gun

Security Girl: Hand it over

Trevon gives her his gun

Security Girl: Big homie in the back.

Big Homie: what's good homie

Trevon: Tired i just came from practice.

Big Homie: I wanna talk to you about some shit.

Trevon: What's up?

Big Homie: How long you plan on doing this shit. I mean you have a bright future.

Trevon: I don't know. My folks from the slumbs from the seven ward. I am just trying to get it.

Big Homie: Man I know this gonna sound crazy. This money don't mean nothing to me. I just wanna see a young nigga like you make it. This street money ain't nothing to $120 million dollar contract in the NBA.

Trevon: *Stares at Big Homie in disbelief*

Damn Big Homie, I will give it up soon homie

Big Homie: Man just think about it. Here go your package.

Trevon gets his gun going out the door. Trevon rides listening to music and thinking.

Trevon wakes up late, overslept, missed school and has 20 missed calls

Trevon: what's good son. I just woke up. I have about 20 missed calls. I be there in about an hour.

Trevon: I got to call Coach

Phone rings

Coach: Hello, man where the hell you at? You didn't come to school and we have a game tonight.

Trevon: I know Coach. I am sorry. I woke up late. I will be there.

Coach: I have to talk to you when you get here.

Trevon: Okay I apologize

Coach: Okay I will see you at 4:00

SCENE CHANGE

Dominique: Hey what's wrong?

Steven: I am worried about my homie. He didn't show up to school.

Dominique: Don't yall have a game tonight?

Steven: Yes, coach is really stricked when you don't show up for school on game day.

Dominique: Hopefully he show up. Not to change the subject but my dad is ready to meet you.

Steven: He is? Is he mean?

Dominique: He not, he just kind of over protective about me. I am his only daughter and only child.

Steven: Kool.

Dominique: Then you can asked, him if you can take me out to prom.

Steven: Take you to Prom

Dominique: If you wanna take me, you have to ask my pops

Steven: Ok. *looking worried*

SCENE CHANGE

Coach: Trevon, what's going on man you acting different son. You got a lot of opportunity here, don't blow it.

Trevon: I know Coach, I just over sleep.

Coach: Get dress

SCENE CHANGE

Cougar basketball win again 22- 0 undefeated

All players talking in locker room after the game

Steven: Hey Trevon, Can I catch a ride home with you after the game?

Trevon: Yes,

SCENE CHANGE

Steven and Trevon riding and talking on the way home

Trevon: Yea bro, me and Coach talk before the game.

Steven: That's good yo. I have recruiting letters coming in by the dozens.

Trevon: Me to, man you want something to eat? I am hungry.

Steven: Yes,

Trevon: Ok,

Trevon, Dam, police behind us!

Steven: What's wrong do you have your license?

Trevon: Yea, just don't move a lot these cops crazy.

Cop: Hey gentlemen, you have your licenses, insurance and registration.

Trevon: Yes, sir.

Trevon hands over all the stuff

Officer: Ok I will be right back. Where are yall coming from?

Trevon: High school game sir.

Trevon: Hey, don't act nervous, I forgot I have something in my glovebox.

Steven: Oh man, I can't go to jail. My momma is gonna kill me bruh.

Trevon: Just stay calm homie.

Officer: Ok Trevon, could you step out, put your hand behind your back. You have the right to remain silent.

Trevon: What I do?

Officer: You have a warrant for a ticket.

Officer: Excuse me, do you have a license? Steven: No Sir.

Officer: Well I will have to tow this vehicle

Steven: Ok

Officer: You have a cell phone, call for a ride.

Steven: Ok Sir

Officers talking that kid seems very nervous.

Officer: Do you have any guns, drugs or alcohol in the vehicle?

Steven: No Sir, why would we do that?

Officer: We gonna take a look around.

Officer looking in vehicle and finds brown bag in glove box and in the trunk a bag with $70,000.

Officer: You're under arrest too. You have the right to remain silent *Two different cars bring them to the station.*

SCENE CHANGE

Kids at school talking

School kids: Hey Dominique

Dominique: Yea

School Kid #1: Hey you know Steven and Trevon in jail?

Dominique: For what!?

School Kid #1: We was wishing you knew?

Dominique: I didn't know they was locked up

Slim walks up

Slim: I heard Trevon got pop ha?

Dominique: What?

Slim: Yea Trevon from my hood. He got that work, it caught up with him.

School Kid #2: So his parents didn't buy his car?

Slim laughs

Slim: Trevon don't have any parents. He has his own apartment. His parents died when he was young. Homie be getting that money.

School Kid #1: Wow

Dominque: So Steven got caught up with Trevon, he don't sell drugs right?

Slim: No, Steven don't sell drugs. I guess he was in the wrong place at the wrong time.

Dominique call Steven mom.

Dominique: Hello Mrs. Janice. This is Dominque, I heard Steven is in trouble. Did you talk to him?

Janice: Yes, his bond is $250,000 and Trevon one is $300,000. I don't have that type of money. My child life in ruined.

Dominique: Please tell him to call me on my cellphone.

Janice: I have to put money on his books first.

Dominque: Okay I have twenty bucks if that will help.

Janice: God got this. My child name will get cleared.

Dominque: ok anyway I can help I will. Talk to you later.

Janice: Ok bye.

SCENE CHANGE

Coach in the locker room talking to the team before the game

Coach: We have two players that was important to our team. We can't feel sorry for ourselves, we have to fight two games left. One game at a time. Push the ball after every basket we make.

Team: EVERYBODY ON ONE "LETS GET EM"

SCENE CHANGE

In jail

Steven: Hey trustee, I need you to take something down the hall for me to Dorm D.

Trustee: That gonna be two stamped envelopes younging.

Steven: OK

Trustee: What you in for

Steven: Drug Charge

Trustee: They have a lot of snitches around here. Keep your business to yourself and last don't be afraid to fight because they gonna test you.

Trustee: What's your name?

Steven: Steven Dupree

Trustee: You knows a Richard Dupree?

Steven: Yes, that's my Pop

Trustee: Yes, he's an old military vet. I did desert storm with him.

Steven: Yes, he's still deployed.

Trustee: I got, you tell your dad fast lane Rick said hello. Tell him i use to be the diver.

SCENE CHANGE

Hot Rod: Hey Trevon, I heard you was on your way in here.

Trevon: Yea man, they caught me slipping. They got me fuck up.

Hot Rod: I hate to hear that homie. I heard yall was about to win another state championship and yall was like undefeated or something.

Trevon: Yea Homie we were balling.

Hot Rod: Are you gonna bond out?

Trevon: I don't know yet? I don't have a bond yet. Plus, I got a lil probation hold.

Hot Rod: They will give you one when you see the Magistrate Judge in the morning.

SCENE CHANGE

Dominique: Hey Ms Iceland how its going today?

Teacher: I am good, What's going on my favorite student.

Dominique smiles

Dominique: Can we talk? I haven't seen my cycle and I am fearful I might be pregnant. I am scared of a lot of things.

Teacher: Well Dominique, you can buy a pregnancy test.

Dominique: I might finish Valedictorian; so I am going to college. My dad would be disappointed and the father could be in jail for a long time if I am.

Teacher: Oh Dominique, I am here for you. I got pregnant at 14 teen so I can relate baby. But go get the pregnancy test and then go see a physician.

Dominique: My father would kill me if he found out.

Teacher: No Dominique, he would be upset at first. He loves you. So he would forgive. He will be proud of his daughter graduating, straight As.

Dominique: You think?

Teacher: Yes.

Dominique: Ok

Dominique going in bathroom then looking at pregnancy test, positive, then crying and in room worrying while music is playing

SCENE CHANGE

OG: Hey younging. It could be rough in here sometime and where you could be headed.

Trevon: My whole life been rough and scary OG. My mom and pop got killed in a robbery when I was three. The robbers spared me but killed my mom and pop. I was in the house with two dead parents for two days OG before they found me that's why I aint scared of nothing OG.

OG: Damn I hear you homie. I was just giving you heads up.

Trevon: Nice looking out.

SCENE CHANGE

Sermon

Thomas: Pastor, sermon on family was great Tasha: Yes, bible study was wonderful.

Thomas: What you cooking? I'm starved.

Tasha: I have a taste for some baked fish, Caribbean rice and veggies.

SCENE CHANGE

CRASH

A colliding drunk driver runs a red light and kills Thomas and Tasha after Bible Study.

One month before Dominique graduate.

SCENE CHANGE

Two officer go to Dominique's house and break the news to her. Show Dominique crying in distress.

SCENE CHANGE

Dominique friend Teacher and Steven mom get the news and try to console her.

Dominique: I didn't get to tell him I was pregnant.

Dominique faints then falls and take her to the emergency room

SCENE CHANGE

Dominique envisions her mom telling her dad, Thomas, she was pregnant. Thomas smile, I can't wait my first grandchild.

Janice: Hello, I am glad you called. I have some bad news Steven: What ma, everybody alright?

Janice: No Dominique parents got killed in a car accident.

Steven: NOOO!!! She don't have no one.

Janice: Yes, she do. God son and she's moving in with me.

Steven: Thanks mom Thanks. I go for bond reduction tomorrow.

Janice: Just pray son. Say your prayers boy.

Steven: I will ma

SCENE CHANGE

Principal and Coach talk

Principle Harvey: Hey Coach, big game tonight.

Coach: yes, it is, we're under manned.

Coach: But were not going to feel sorry for ourselves.

Principal Harvey: We have something or someone that might inspire.

SCENE CHANGE

Students and teachers wear win for Dominique T-shirts in support of her losing her dad and step mom in a car accident.

Dominique high school wins the basketball state championship.

Dominique's mother in law gets diagnosed with lupus.

SCENE CHANGE

Narrator, speaks in "Dominique voice" I graduated high school as a single parent and started college. Young, vulnerable, and lonely. I made a mistake and dated a guy name Cardell.

Cardell: Hey you wanna study tonight by your place or mine?

Dominique: I can't do that again. I told you I have a boyfriend that locked up.

Cardell: Is he here now? Besides, we have a project to study for

Dominique: I will study alone

Cardell: Please I will fail if you don't help me

Cardell: Ok we can study at the coffee shop

Dominique: We can ONLY do school work. You're a nice guy but I am in love with someone else.

Cardell: That's kool, I understand. Classmates only from now on... Dominique: Can you handle that?

Cardell: I will do my best.

OK! OK! I can please...

Six years later

Dominique is driven to pick up Steven after getting released Their daughter gets to see her father for the first time.

Jena: Mommy you said my daddy is tall, right?

Dominique: Yes, why you asked Jena?

Jena: I don't want a short daddy.

Dominique: *laughs*

Well we will get to see in a hour.

Steven gets off the bus with bags

Jena runs to him

They all embrace

Steven: It's been a long six years. I am so proud of you Sweet Dominique. You graduate and now your working on your second degree your my inspiration.

Dominique: I know baby now we can be a family. Your mom is waiting. She is cooking your favorite, mustard green and corn bread.

Steven: Yes, my daughter Jena is beautiful.

Dominique: Steven I have something to discuss with you when we make it home.

Steven: What is it baby, let's talk.

Dominique: Well I don't wanna make your time harder… but Steven: BUT! Don't tell me you got pregnant.

Dominique: *Shakes her head*

Steven: Oh! My god, noooooo.

Dominique: I am sorry baby.

Steven: Why you didn't tell me while I was locked up. I could have mentally prepared myself

for this.

Dominique: Baby I am sorry. Can we please still be one family.

Steven: *pauses* yes, we don't have a choice.

Dominique kisses Steven.

SCENE CHANGE

Steven makes it home mom dad and family is awaiting his arrival in celebration.

Janice Oh my. Look at my son.

Steven: I miss you mom

Steven and his mom embrace

Lenord: Come here boy

They embrace

Lenord: Look how you matured.

Steven: It's been a long journey. I appreciate all the money and advice you gave while I was in there, Pop.

Lenord: I appreciate you making it home in one piece. You're my only child.

Steven: Your son aint no punk. I handled mine.

Lenord: Shit I know that

Steven: Pop, how would you feel if your girl had a baby while you was locked up?

Lenord: Son, that's life. She been there for you. She's a good girl she's only human besides you're who she love.

Steven: Yes it's not her fault I got locked.

Lenord: And she was there. She doing big things. Marry her.

Steven: That's what I plan to do…

Lenord: I will holler at you in the house.

Dominique: I have something special plan for you tonight Steven: Really!!

Dominique: I miss you. Your mom is about to say grace let's eat.

Dominique and Steven enjoy the tonight together.

Dominique: I took off from work a couple of days to help you get acclimated and so you, I and the kids could spent time.

Steven: OK, kool baby. I have to get to work soon after I see my P.O. today so I can be a good dad and help you with the kids. Dominique: I just want us to be one beautiful family Steven: Ok as couple romance.

Phone rings as Steven is getting dressed.

Steven: Hey, who is this?... What's good fam?... I am good...ok what time?...ok I am about to go eat out with my girl and we can meet after that...ok bye.

Dominique: Who is that babe?

Steven: The big homie.

Dominique: What he want?

Steven: He say he wanna take me shopping

Dominique: Baby you don't have to take nothing from him. With that come stipulations Steven: No not from me. He knows better. Don't worry baby I can handle myself.

SCENE CHANGE

Trevon is a devote Christian now in prison.

Trevon: Yea, Jesus is everything my brother and we need our higher power to survive temptation when we go back into society and in this situation.

Kendell: You are so right John 1:41 says…

Correctional Officer: Inmate its count time fellows.

Trevon: We can finish this Bible Study after count time

Kendell: Kool

SCENE CHANGE

Steven pulls up to meet Big swag

Big Swag: Look at this nigga looking all swoll and shit.

Steven: *laughs* What's good.

Chuck: *stutters as he talks,* Boy you and Trevon been gone a minute, how long you did?

Steven: Six years

Big Swag: Trevon say he got one year left all he talk about is God and Religion.

Chuck: Yea that's all the jail house talk.

Big Swag: That nigga gonna be back out here thugging.

Steven: I hope not, I am looking for a job.

Big Swag: That's Kool, I just wanna salute you for keeping it real, knowing none of that work was yours for keeping it real to the hood. Here go some bread.

Steven: I appreciate it although I can't take this. I mean I just did what any real nigga would do.

Big Swag: You don't owe me anything this for you and your family.

Steven: No stipulations behind this ha?

Big Swag: No besides you and Trevon made me rich when yall was winning those State

Championships. I bet on yall every game with other dealers $20,000 a game.

Steven: Wow!

Big Swag: Yep. Let's go to the mall nigga

SCENE CHANGE

Dominique and Stacey talk at the café during lunch.

Stacey: SO how have it been since your man came home?

Dominique: It's been wonderful.

Stacey: How he feel about your situation?

Dominique: He learn to accept my baby. We are one big family no problems. He's been really looking for a job but it's hard for a convicted felon.

Stacey: Yes, that's how it was for my brother. It took months to find a job.

Dominique: I got us until he get straight.

Stacey: are you excited about graduation coming up

Dominique: yes, I can't wait, I am done with school now a master's degree is good enough for me on my journey

Stacey: Let's have a graduation party and you can invite your coworkers and friends and family, of course.

Dominique: That's a good idea. Let me talk to Steven about it and we can take it from there.

Stacey: OK

SCENE CHANGE

After taking Steven shopping Big Swag and Steven talk in the car.

Steven: Thanks very much Big Homie

Big Swag: No problem. I know how hard it is after a long Jose. I did a couple of them.

Steven: Yea you did a long Jose when I was real young.

Big Swag: Yea I did 7 in the Federal Penitentiary. So that's why I got a proposition for you get you a job. And come get some off this street money too. I mean it's hard for a convict to get a good job anyway.

Steven: I couldn't find time between my girl kids and work, I can't manage.

Big Swag I would guide you.

Steven: I never sold dope before.

Big Swag: That's great, I will show you the ropes. And how to make plenty money. Just think about it.

Steven: I will let you know.

SCENE CHANGE

Dominique meets her baby daddy to get her child.

Cardell: All his stuff is in the bag.

Dominique: OK

Cardell: I miss you

Dominique: Stop my man is home now don't disrespect me are him. Cardell: You mean your baby daddy home. So what! I am your baby daddy too.

Dominique: Cardell don't start; besides I got to go.

Cardell: Hey I don't want that nigga around Cardell Jr. period. I don't want that jail bird in my child life.

Dominique: Oh well, he will be. Whether you like it or not. Bye *Dominique pulls off in the car as Cardell stares in anger.*

SCENE CHANGE

Jena: Daddy, you're a good daddy. Why did you have to go to a bad place like jail?

Steven: Because wrong place at the wrong time. Sometimes friends are not really your friends. Besides, I thought about you every day I was gone.

Jena: I am so happy to have a daddy.

Steven: And I am happy to have a beautiful daughter.

SCENE CHANGE

Work on line in kitchen in prison

Trevon: What you want my brother? A lil cabbage and some rice?

Black OG: I won't never see society again; so, I have to live through young brothers like you Trevon.

Trevon: Black OG. I will do my best not to let you down with Jesus help and never give up on your freedom. God has something special planned for you.

Fight breaks out in prison kitchen

Black OG: These dudes do this, every day.

Trevon: I hope we don't go back on lockdown.

Black OG: I have something to tell you during bible study tonight.

Trevon: ok

SCENE CHANGE

Stacey: Baby its getting tighter and more difficult for you.

Chris: Yea, they cut me down to 40 hours now and a lay off is apparent.

Stacey: I can get another job.

Chris: Where at baby? You work enough. No baby.

Stacey: One night a week at the strip club.

Chris: Hell no! I would go work at McDonalds before I let you do that.

Stacey: I can make two grand a night.

Chris: NO! I don't wanna talk about it again.

Stacey: So we gonna lose everything we work for because of your pride?

Chris: NO, I have never seen that side of you. And I don't wanna see you in that dark light. You're my wife, not a stripper.

Stacey: Chris, I will get three jobs if I have to.

SCENE CHANGE

Homeless man asks Janice for a dollar as she is getting out of the car at the Hospital. She had an appointment for her lupus. She gives him twenty dollars.

Doctor: Hello Ms. Janice, how are you doing?

Janice: I am doing well.

Doctor: Any symptoms?

Janice: No just headaches at night.

Doctor: Headaches late night. Are those headaches repetitive or every once in a while?

Janice: Once or twice a week.

Doctor: Okay, I have your results.

Janice: Good News Lord

Doctor: Your recovery has been everything but amazing. All of the test we ran show no sign of lupus.

Janice: Thank you Jesus.

Doctor: Although we still want you to come back in a month for a check-up.

Janice: Thank you Lord.

SCENE CHANGE

Cardell is at a sports bar drinking and talking to some friends. He is drinking excessively; cheers after team scores

Cardell: My team won, Shots for everybody, bartender.

Bartender: OK

Cardell: Hey Bobby, you single right?

Bobby: Yea

Cardell: How would you feel is a convicted felon was hanging around your child.

Bobby: I wouldn't like it, he might harm my child. Who is this chump? Depends on what he went to jail for?

Cardell: My baby mother baby daddy just got out of prison. I don't want that chump around my son. Period.

Bobby: Sound like you and baby mom need to have a conversation.

Cardell: I will try that, but she stubborn bro.

Bobby: Women don't like when men out think them. Shoot if that don't work file for custody of your son.

Cardell: That's a good idea, Thanks for the advice.

SCENE CHANGE

Steven stops by his mom, Janice's house.

Steven knocks on the door Janice: Who it is?

Steven: It's me Mom, Steven.

Janice: Hey Son, How's it going?

Steven: Still looking for a job.

Janice: Be patient, its gonna work out.

Steven: So how did your doctor visit go?

Janice: It went great. The doctor said I am recovery faster than any patient he ever had.

Steven hugs his mom.

Steven: That's great!

Janice: And he released me to go back to work.

Steven: Dominique is gonna be happy to hear this good news. Her graduation party will be soon.

SCENE CHANGE

Stacey applies for a job at a Gentlemen's Club.

Stacey: Hello I am here to meet with Big Craig. My name is Stacey Daggs.

Receptionist: OK… Craig you have a Stacey Daggs here for an interview.

Ok babe he is waiting on you in his office.

Big Craig: Hello Mrs. Daggs

Stacey: Hello

Big Craig: Have you ever work as a professional dancer?

Stacey: No I haven't although I have been on several dance teams as a teenager.

Big Craig: *Full of laughter* Baby this club is far different than those dance teams, trust me. I will give you a job as a shot girl for a couple of weeks.

Stacey: Ok I will take it!

Big Craig: This way you can learn and if you like it, we will let you dance. My girls is gonna train you up.

Stacey: Thanks, when do I start?

Big Craig: Fridays is one of our busiest night. You can start then, I will see you then.

SCENE CHANGE

Bible Study ending in prison

Black OG: Hey Trevon, remember I wanted to chat with you.

Trevon: Yea OG?

Black OG: The big dog wanna holla at you Trevon: At me, why? I don't do gangs.

Black OG: Well you going home soon. We need a connect to the outside.

Trevon: For what?

Black OG: Everything; coke, heroin, pills…

Trevon: I will hook yall up with some good people on the outside. But I am trying to live right. I'm not coming back here.

Black OG: Just holler at the big dog. He wanna meet tomorrow on the wreck yard.

Trevon: Ok kool, I'm standing on my morals.

Black OG: Remember this is an organization. They don't like the words no and I can't your freedom and life can be at stake youngin.

Trevon: Why me?

Black OG: Because you been solid from day one homie. That's why. This is high praise.

SCENE CHANGE

Dominique cooking at home as Steven walks in.

Steven: Hey honey, how was your day?

Dominique: It was good baby.

Steven: What's wrong?

Dominique: Nothing just ready for this school stuff to be over with. I am ready to focus on my family and my career. Having a masters degree is enough education for me.

Steven: Yes, baby it is. I have a couple of interviews set up. And mommy got good news from the Doctor. She's doing great and she's been released to go back to work.

Dominique: That's great! I can't wait to see momma. I will call her later when I finish cooking.

SCENE CHANGE

Stacey First day at the strip club.

Red Lipstick: Alright baby. Here's the rules and guidelines.

One. Never give out your real number.

Two. Tell these niggas anything they wanna hear to get their money.

Three. Watch me and you will make plenty money ***laughs***

Stacey: How long have you been doing this?

Red Lipstick: Six years but I am a realtor in the day time. I own several properties. Let's get some money girl.

SCENE CHANGE

Trevon in jail, on the yard with Big Slack.

Trevon: Hey Big Dog

Slack: What good lil homie. Just call me Slack.

Trevon: Ok kool

Slack: The reason I wanted to talk to you was I need real niggas on the outside to make my operation work. I have done my homework on you, your rep check clean on the street and in here.

Trevon: What you need from me homie?

Slack: I need consistency on all the product like pills, heroin, coke and good.

Trevon: Big Slack, how about I hook you up with a couple of quality people from my neighborhood?

Slack: No I don't wanna deal with no one I never met before.

Trevon: I can respect that but I changed homie. I am going out there with a clean slate. I don't wanna come back here.

Slack: Nigga, everybody changed when they in here and they get outside and they see nobody don't give a fuck about a convict getting out of prison!

Trevon: I got to do the right thing for me.

Slack: Hey nigga!! I am tired of playing with you. I gave you a opportunity do what I ask you.

Or your skinny ass won't make it home.

Trevon: ***Stares at Slack in fear***

SCENE CHANGE

Steven: What's good homie?

Big Swag: Man, it's war on these streets. One of my little people got shot on 33rd last night.

Steven: Damn who?

Big Swag: Lil Toby. It's not looking good for him.

Steven: What that streets saying.

Big Swag: I already know who did it and why. What happen in the streets stays in the streets.

Steven: Word!

SCENE CHANGE

Big Swag and Steven riding

Big Swag: I am glad your mom is doing well fam. I lost my mom last year things haven't been the same since.

Steven: I will share my mom with you fam.

Big Swag: I appreciate that if I go to spoiling your mom with gifts, don't start feeling some type of way.

Steven: *Laughing.* I am not

Big Swag: I wish I could get out this street life like you, homie. But I am too far in. You got a good girl sweet mom, two beautiful kids.

Steven: I lost a lot of valuable time though in the joint.

Big Swag: Oh shit!

Steven: What?

Big Swag: Damn police behind us. Stay calm bro.

Police: Driver license, insurance and registration Big Swag: Here you go officer. How you doing today?

Police: I am doing well. Where yall going?

Big Swag: We going see a friend in the hospital.

Police: Hang tight, I will be right back.

Steven: Man, I am about to run.

Big Swag: Be cool fool. I am clean. If he ask to search the car, then you can run. I got two hundred thousand in the trunk I forgot about.

Police: Here you go Mr. Jones. Get that back break light fixed on the right. Yall have a good day.

Big Swag: Thanks Officer.

SCENE CHANGE

Chris and Stacey eating out at a restaurant.

Receptionist: Two?

Stacey: Yes, only two.

Chris: I am hungry.

Stacey: Me too, I am going freshen up. Tell her I want a lemonade.

Chris: OK

Two chicks walk in talking about strip clubs and money sitting across from Chris Passion: Girl some of them dudes wanna stalk and not throw money.

Red Lipstick: I know they should throw they ass out.

Red Lipstick sees Stacey and speaks.

Red Lipstick: Hey girl, look at Lingerie.

Stacey: Hi

Red Lipstick: Girl you have to work tonight?

Stacey: No girl

Chris: Lingerie?

Stacey: Baby that's my coworkers.

Chris: Those are strippers. You did what I told you not to do tell your coworkers give you a ride home.

SCENE CHANGE

Black OG: Damn youngin'. Slack was very upset after yall meeting.

Trevon: I know... I told him I was willing to help...

Black OG: God is gonna work this out...

Trevon: Man talk to that dude. I don't want no trouble I am just trying to go home bro...
Black OG: I will do my best ... watch yourself until I get this squared away.

SCENE CHANGE

Steven: Man why you riding around with two hundred thousand dollars in the trunk of your car.

Big Swag: Man, I was just messing with you homie. I just wanted to see you sweat.

Steven: Nigga don't play like that. Now I'm gonna have to throw these under wear away.

Because I don't want my girl to see these shit stains in my draws.

Big Swag and Steven laugh...

Steven: Man let's see if the homie all right.

SCENE CHANGE

Dominique leaves court and Cardell walks up from behind to discuss her son.

Dominique: Don't do that you scared me. What do you want?

Cardell: I want custody of my son. And if not I'll see you in court. I can't even see my son when I want?

Dominique: Cardell That's a lie. You get visitation every other weekend.

Cardell: That's not enough besides I don't want my son around a jail bird. I will take my son, you're an unfit mother.

Dominique: How am I unfit!! I will see you in court.

SCENE CHANGE

Stacey made it home. Chris took his clothes and left a note on the table. Stacey cries

SCENE CHANGE

"Cell phone call"

Steven: Hello…. Yes, this is him… Yes, I can drive a forklift. Yes, I will be there for six am.

Thank you!!

SCENE CHANGE

Cardell: Hello, I am here to see Mike Moleny

Receptionist: Ok, let me let him know you're here.

Hey Mike Cardell Richard is in the lobby.

You can go in the back.

Cardell: Hello Mike

Attorney Mike: Hi Mike, it's been awhile.

Cardell: Yes, I been working and dealing with a crazy baby momma.

Attorney Mike: Don't sound like nothing I can't handle.

Cardell: Well I want to get custody of my son. My ex got a boyfriend who is her first baby daddy who just got out of prison. I don't want that criminal around my son.

Attorney Mike: Can you prove her unfit? Does she do drugs? Can you prove the environment your son live in is dangerous or unhealthy?

Cardell: No she never did drugs. She do everything right. I don't know dude and don't trust him around my kid.

Attorney Mike: Well the best thing you can do at this moment is file for joint custody. We have to be able to prove they live together. And dig in baby daddy background to prove him to be a dangerous guy.

Cardell: So this will be a long process?

Attorney Mike: Yes, these custody battle sometime take years!

SCENE CHANGE

Dominique knocking on Stacey door

Stacey: Hey Friend

Dominique: Hey girl, how are you doing? I had to ride to your house to come check on you because bitch don't wanna answer the phone.

Stacey: I been going through it.

Dominique: What's wrong?

Stacey: I started working in a strip club… Chris found out and left my ass… he won't answer none of my calls

Dominique: Friend what was you thinking about?

Stacey: I was trying to make some extra money for us. He got laid off his job.

Dominique: Awwwww sister, he will be back if he love you. In the meanwhile, you got to get yourself together.

Stacey: You excited about your graduation.

Dominique: Yes, I am but my baby daddy tripping. He want me to give him my son.

Stacey: What? Is he crazy?

Dominique: Talking about he don't want his son around no jail bird.

Stacey: Cardell tripping. When his whole family got bad jackets and his brother has five life sentences for killing those five people in that crack house.

Dominique: Yep, he the only one that made it out of his family. Well enough about him.

Steven got a job girl. He called excited today. I am glad too.

Stacey: that's great girl…

SCENE CHANGE

Life management class in prison with Trevon, Kendell and several others

Timothy Smith: Hello gentlemen, my name is Timothy Smith. But please call me Tim. As y'all know you can't go home unless you complete this life management class. I have a lot of informative information to help you guys in class for when you all assimilate back in to society. Any questions?

Kendell: Yes, what would someone like you know how hard it is after doing a bid. Most of us is institutionalized going back to the unwelcoming world.

Tim: Good question. Well I did a ten year bid for robbery. I just look like this. I had to change the way I think. I did four years in college and got my Bachelor in Education. And now it's harder for y'all now than it was for me. Anyone wanna guess why?

Trevon: More guns and drug more temptation?

Tim: That's part of it but that not much different. Internet, social media.

Facebook Mark Zuckerberg is a billionaire.

Instagram Kevin Sistrom is a billionaire from their creation.

Snapchat, Evan Spiegel was a billionaire at 26.

See they put these distractions out there so we can't focus on what we need to. What's the thing they put on the internet to make you lose focus.

Classmate #1: ASS! Plenty ASS!

Class laughs

Tim: Yes

Trevon: Cars, jewelry, fighting

Tim: Guns, drugs, everything but education, family and God. One off the things I had to do is know that I was gonna be a outcast in my hood. Dudes gonna say you done got soft, you aint dealing and killing, riding no mo…Are you ready to show your family and friends you really changed? Some of them is really gonna challenge you.

Inmate #2: Mr. Tim, the streets is all I know. I never had a job and I am 31 years old. The only way some of your family and friends know how to show love is to give you a AK and a bag and say get your money.

Tim: I faced all of that I was well known in my hood. But I said no homies I love y'all but I changed and I love God. I got a job washing dishes then got in school went to college and work. I didn't have time for bullshit. I wanna see you guys live, survive and be successful.

SCENE CHANGE

Cardell riding around, listening to music and drinking

Music "I see death around the corner…"

Steven pull up at the gas station to pump gas

Steven: Hey Rondo

Rondo: Steven? How long you been out fool?

Steven: Two months now…

Rondo: It's good to see you, what you up to?

Steven: Working fam.

Rondo: That's good homie stay free.

Steven: That's what I plan to do. Stay up.

Lemme get $15 on pump four

Clerk: $15 on pump four, the soft drink too?

Steven: Yes

Clerk: $16.14 cent

Steven is pumping gas when a car pulls up Shooter: Hey Homie, you left your gas cap open *Fires two shots, striking Steven.*

SCENE CHANGE

Hospital scene with family and friends Janice: Where is my baby? My only child Lord!

Dominique: Mom, he is in surgery.

Janice: Can someone explain to me what happened?

Big Swag: They say he was pumping gas at the store, a car pulled up and started firing. Ms., Janice we promise we will find out who did this…

Janice: I don't want more violence.

Big Swag: We will talk to you all later. Dominique keep us informed.

Dominique: Okay I will

Janice: His father is on his way...

Doctor: Okay the surgery went well although Steven is unresponsive and in a coma. All we can do is play the waiting game and keep him comfortable. We can only allow one at a time to see him. And one person can stay overnight.

Dominique: You can go mommy Janice.

Detective: Hello. Ms. Dominique, do you know anyone that would hurt Steven Dominique: Besides my baby daddy, no.

Detective: Did you say your baby daddy?

Dominique: Yes, he didn't want Steven around his son.

Detective: We will follow up on it what's his name?

Dominique: Cardell Scott

Detective: Any arguments with these two? Dominique: No Sir

Detective: Any threats or known enemies?

Dominique: No Sir

Detective: Where were you when this took place?

Dominique: I was at the daycare when I got the call...

Detective: Ok we will be in touch and I hope and pray he makes it ok...

Dominique and Janice is sleep in waiting room area in the A.M. as Lenord arrives...
Lenord: Hey you two you can go home and get some rest.

Janice: Lenord, I am glad you're here.

Dominique: Ms. Janice, you can leave. I'll stay…

Janice: Ok I will pick Jena up from Stacey and bring her to school…

Lenord: Whoever did this to my child is gonna pay…

Janice: All we can do is wait and pray…. *Crying…*

Lenord: *"Phone rang" What when were? I just received a phone call. saying the person who did this too my son Cardell Scott shot and killed him self before officers could get him out the house.*

Detective #1: Call the corona he's dead…

Detective #2: Wow! What a cowardly act…

SCENE CHANGE

Chuck: Big Swag that fool Cardell blowed his brain out before the police could get him.

Big Swag: Damn I wanted to be the one to do that… That worthless piece of scumbag is pussy.

Chuck: Steven Daddy, Mr. Lenord flew in town…

Big Swag: Lord, I know we done a lot of wrong on the streets. Please let Steven pull through… Take me Lord, he deserve to live…

Dominique stares at Steven and reminisces on their past happiness; while he is still in coma

Trevon: Hey, long time no see

Dominique: Trevon!! You're out, it's a blessing to see you.

Trevon: I am happy to be out but not under these circumstances.

Dominique: I been praying every day that God give us back Steven.

Lenord: Trevon, You're home. He's been in a coma for over a week now.

Trevon: Yes, sir. I came straight here and I am not leaving until my brother is out of this coma.

Lenord: Thanks for the support. You just got out of prison and you're here.

Leonard: I had received a call earlier that the person that did this to my son blew his brains out.

Trevon: That dude crazy I will continue to pray my brother make it threw this.

Dominique: WOW! That dude crazy.

Lenord: Dee go home, get you a bite to eat and see the kids. Me and Trevon will be here. You have been here a week.

Dominique: Ok Mr. Lenord, I will be back tomorrow.

Chris knocks on Stacey door.

Stacey: Who is it?

Chris: It's Chris.

Stacey: Hey,, What are you doing here?

Chris: Can we talk?

Stacey: I don't have that much time… I have to bring Dominique her kids. She has a lot going on right now.

Chris: A lot going on like what?

Stacey: Where you been? Cardell shot Steven then Cardell blow his brains out and … Steven been in a coma for two weeks.

Chris: Wow! My heart go out to her.

Stacey: So, I have been sheltering the kids from all this plus working. I been pretty busy.

Chris: … I got a good job. It's for a computer firm

Stacey: Well good for you

Jena: Ms. Stacey, can I have a candy?

Stacey: Yes.

Chris: Stacey I miss you

Stacey: I miss you too… I apologize I was just trying to help us… I was wrong for doing that.

Chris: I accept your apology.

Stacey: I will call you later so we can talk. Let me bring Dominique her kids…

SCENE CHANGE

Steven moves and calls for his mom, he starts to come out of coma

Nurse: Mr. Steven

Steven: Ma ma

Trevon: Steven!! Steven!!

Steven: Trevon what you doing here?

Trevon: Man I love you boy. You was in a coma, I will be right back.

Nurse: That's right. I will have the doctor come see you… and explain what's going on
        Trevon: Mr. Lenord, he's awoke.

Lenord: Oh My...

Lenord hurries to room to see Steven.

Steven: What's up daddy. What are you doing, am I dreaming?

Steven and Lenord laugh

Trevon: No you're not dreaming bro.

Lenord: God is amazing. Let me call Dominique and your mother. They will be ecstatic.

SCENE CHANGE

Two Weeks later Sweet Dominique accepts masters degree at her college graduation.

Graduation host: Sweet Dominique She a straight a student who acquired her masters degree. Dominique please speak to our graduation class.

Crowd claps

Dominique: Thank you I wanna Thank God, my family and friends, my classmates and instructors that motivated me when I didn't feel like it... I wanna personalize with you all for a moment.

Dominique pauses and points to heaven. I want to thank my mother Yvette Lovely. The day I was born the doctor said to her and my dad. One of us wasn't going to make it. She made the ultimate sacrifice a mother can make for a child she told my day I lived twenty nine years she deserves to live. Today I am blessed with two kids and a fiance. I lost my brother Tete to gun violence straight A student. He didn't deserve to die so early. My dad and stepmom both got killed in a car crash. I got pregnant at the age of seventeen. I said all this to say, if I can accomplish this degree. After facing all these obstacles you can't use excuses you can't let your circumstances define you. This degree is for my spiritual family that allowed me to enjoy these accomplishments with my physical fam.

THE END

Dominique and Steven get married

Steven becomes a youth counselor

Dominique becomes the CEO of a Fortune 500 company called Global Telecommunication

Shots of marriage ceremony

Steven in tie and talking to the youth

Author – Will-Chill

11/17/15 12:15 am

Finish date January 27, 2007

Author Will Holmes January 27,2007 of project Sweet Dominique.

Steven shares his life and story helping dis advantage kids in New Orleans as a youth counselor. Steven Marry Dominique and live happy ever after.

Printed in the United States
By Bookmasters